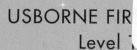

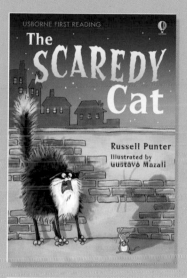

USBORNE FIRST READING

The
**SCAREDY
Cat**

Russell Punter
Illustrated by
Gustavo Mazali

USBORNE FIRST READING

The
**Mouse's
Wedding**

Retold by Mairi Mackinnon
Illustrated by Frank Endersby

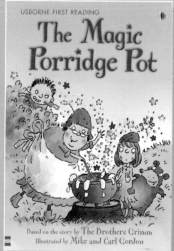

USBORNE FIRST READING

**The Magic
Porridge Pot**

Based on the story by The Brothers Grimm
Illustrated by Mike and Carl Gordon

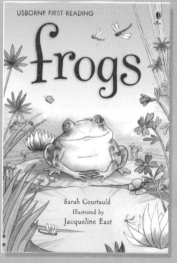

USBORNE FIRST READING

frogs

Sarah Courtauld
Illustrated by
Jacqueline East

Thumbelina

Based on a story by
Hans Christian Andersen

Retold by
Susanna Davidson

Illustrated by Petra Brown

Reading Consultant: Alison Kelly
Roehampton University

Once, there was a woman who wanted a child.

She wanted one more than anything else in the world.

2

At last, she went to a fairy
for help.

"Here is a magic seed,"
said the fairy.

"Put it in a flower pot, and see what happens."

The seed grew into a beautiful red-gold flower.

The woman bent and kissed it.

And the petals of the flower began to open.

Inside was a tiny girl, no bigger than a thumb.

I'll call you Thumbelina.

The woman made her a
bed out of a walnut shell.
It had rose petals for sheets.

Each day, Thumbelina
floated on a tulip leaf in a
saucer of water.

When she felt lonely, she
sang to herself.

One night, a large, lumpy
toad crept through the
open window...

She snatched Thumbelina
as she slept.

"What a pretty wife you'll make for my son," she croaked.

Her son grinned and gazed
at Thumbelina, happily.

11

"We'll keep her on a water lily in the middle of the stream," said Mother Toad.

"She'll never escape."

Thumbelina woke to see four large eyes, blinking at her.

Then a large webbed hand reached for her.

"No!" cried Thumbelina,
trying to get away.

"Meet your future
husband," said Mother Toad.

"But I don't want to marry a toad," Thumbelina sobbed.

The fishes in the stream heard her cries.

15

The toads left for food and
the fish swam closer.

They nibbled and
nibbled at the water lily.

And it was swished away
by the stream.

I'm free!

Thumbelina floated for
days, past villages and
wide green fields.

Butterflies fluttered around
her. Birds twittered and sang
to her.

The sun shone on the water
so that it glittered like gold.

But, all the time, a big brown beetle was watching her.

He swooped down and grabbed her in his claws.

19

"Yuck!" said the lady
beetles. "She's ugly. Take
her away!"

20

So the beetle dropped her in a field.

For tiny Thumbelina, the field was like a forest.

There she lived, all summer.

She wove herself a bed with
blades of grass, and hung up
a leaf to stop the rain.

She sucked honey from
flowers and drank the
dew from their leaves.

Swallows swooped and
dived around her, so she
never felt alone.

Then winter came and the swallows left. Thumbelina shivered with cold.

"What are you doing out here?" asked a field mouse.

She took Thumbelina back
to her snug little home.

"We'll have a visitor soon,"
said the field mouse. "He's a
rich and clever mole."

26

When the mole came,
he talked about his life
underground.

"I never go outside," he
said. "Come and see my
splendid house."

Thumbelina went with him
down a dark tunnel.

In the middle of the tunnel
lay a bird. He had fallen
through a hole in the roof.

28

"Oh! Is he dead?" asked
Thumbelina.

"Yes," replied Mole. "If
swallows don't fly away for
winter, they die of cold."

That night, Thumbelina
crept back to the swallow.

She covered him with a
carpet of hay.

"Goodbye!" she said, thinking how sweetly the swallows sang all summer.

But when she put her head on his breast, she heard a, "*Thump*! *Thump*! *Thump*!"

"He's not dead. He's frozen," she realized.

The next night, Thumbelina crept back to see the bird again.

His eyes were open, but he was very weak.

"I'll keep you warm
and take care of you,"
said Thumbelina.

"Thank you," whispered the swallow.

Each night, Thumbelina brought him water and seeds from the field mouse's store.

By springtime, when the sun warmed the earth, the swallow was well again.

"Come with me," he said. "We can fly away to the green woods."

"I can't," said Thumbelina.
"I think the field mouse would
be sad if I left."

So the swallow flew up
out of the tunnel and soared
into the sky, alone.

Thumbelina missed the swallow. She longed to go outside again.

"Cheer up!" said the field mouse. "I have exciting news. Mole wants to marry you."

"But I don't want to marry Mole," gasped Thumbelina.

"Nonsense!" snapped
the field mouse. "Don't be
difficult."

The wedding day was fixed.
Thumbelina was to live deep
under the earth.

She went to say goodbye to
the sky one last time.

"Tweet, tweet," she heard.
She looked up and saw the
swallow.

"Cold winter is coming again," he said. "Come with me to warmer countries."

"Oh, I'll come, I'll come!" cried Thumbelina.

She climbed on his back.
They flew high, over forests
and seas and snow-covered
mountains.

At last, they came to a blue
lake. A dazzling white palace
stood on its sunny shore.

The swallow set Thumbelina
down in a large white flower.

A tiny man stood in the
flower. He had a gold crown
and pale butterfly wings.

I am King of
the Flowers.

He took off his crown and
gave it to Thumbelina.

"Will you stay with me and be Queen of the Flowers?" he asked.

"Yes," said Thumbelina, happy at last.

Then all the other flowers
opened and tiny men and
women appeared.

They each gave
Thumbelina a gift.

Best of all was a beautiful
pair of wings, so she could fly
from flower to flower.

And the swallow swooped
above them all, singing a
joyful song.

USBORNE FIRST READING
Level Four

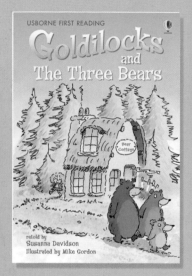

USBORNE FIRST READING

Goldilocks
and
The Three Bears

retold by
Susanna Davidson
Illustrated by Mike Gordon

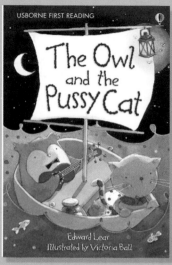

USBORNE FIRST READING

The Owl
and the
Pussy Cat

Edward Lear
Illustrated by Victoria Ball

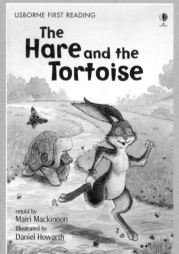

USBORNE FIRST READING

The
Hare and the
Tortoise

retold by
Mairi Mackinnon
Illustrated by
Daniel Howarth

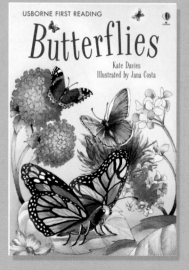

USBORNE FIRST READING

Butterflies

Kate Davies
Illustrated by Jana Costa